THE TIME MACHINE

THE TIME MACHINE

By H. G. Wells

Adapted by Betty Ren Wright
Illustrated by Ivan Powell

Raintree Publishers • Milwaukee • Toronto • Melbourne • London

Library of Congress Number: 81-4097

  2 3 4 5 6 7 8 9 0 85 84 83

Printed in the United States of America.

Library of Congress Cataloging in Publication Data

Wright, Betty Ren.
  The time machine.

  (Raintree short classics)
  Summary: A time traveler voyages into the future
to find the world has been divided into two races.
  [1. Science fiction] I. Wells, H. G. (Herbert
George), 1866-1946. The time machine. II. Powell,
Ivan. III. Title. IV. Series.
  PZ7.W933Ti   [Fic]   81-4097
  ISBN 0-8172-1675-8   AACR2

Emblem on front cover from *Graphic Trade Symbols By
German Designers*, F. H. Ehmcke, Dover Publications

CONTENTS

THE MACHINE

The Time Traveler (for so I will speak of him) was telling us something strange. His gray eyes twinkled, and his usually pale face was rosy. The fire burned brightly, and it was that pleasant time after dinner when thought runs free.

"You must follow me carefully," he said. "The geometry you learned in school is all wrong."

"Isn't that a rather big point to begin with?" asked Filby, who liked to argue.

"The truth is," the Time Traveler went on, "that any object must have four directions. It must have length and breadth and thickness, and it must last. We learn about length and breadth and thickness in school, but the fourth direction — time — is one we cannot see. Still, there is no difference between this fourth one and the other three directions of space except that we are moving along with time and cannot see it. Do you understand?"

"I *think* so," murmured the mayor.

The doctor stared hard at a coal in the fire. "If time is really only another direction of space, why do we think of it as something different? And why can't we move about in time as we can in space? We cannot get away from this moment."

"My dear sir, that is just where you are wrong!" the Time Traveler exclaimed. "We are moving along with time all our lives. Just as we should travel *down* if, for instance, we were born fifty miles above earth."

"Still," I said, "you *can* move about in the height and breadth and thickness of space, but you cannot move about in time."

The Time Traveler became very excited. "That is my great discovery," he said. "You are wrong to say we cannot move about in time. Long ago I began to think about a machine —"

"To travel through time!" exclaimed a very young man.

Filby laughed. "Of all the wild ideas!"

"One could talk to Homer," said the young man. "Or visit the future!"

"Yes, so it seemed to me," said the Time Traveler, "but I never spoke of it until I could prove it."

"Prove it!" I exclaimed. "You can prove that?"

"Let's see your proof," said the doctor.

The Time Traveler smiled at us. Then he walked out of the room, and we heard his slippers shuffling down the hall to his laboratory.

"I wonder what he's got," said the young man.

"Some trick or other," said the doctor.

Filby then began to tell us about a magician he had once seen, but before he had said more than a few words, the Time Traveler came back, and Filby forgot all about his story.

The thing the Time Traveler held in his hand was scarcely larger than a small clock. There was ivory in it, and metal, and something like crystal. He set a small table in front of the fire, and on this table he placed the object. Then he drew up a chair and sat down. The only other thing on the table was a small lamp. There were at least a dozen candles around us, so the room was brightly lit.

We all drew close, on the alert for any kind of trick.

"This little affair," said the Time Traveler, "is only a model. It is my plan for a machine that will travel through time."

"It is beautifully made," said the doctor.

"It took two years to build it," retorted the Time Traveler. "Now, this lever, when pressed, sends the machine gliding into the future, and this other sends it back. This saddle is where the time traveler will sit. Soon I will press the lever, and off the machine will go into the future. Have a good look at it, and look at the table, too. Satisfy yourselves that there is no trick here. I don't want to waste this model and then be told I'm a quack."

He put his finger toward the lever, then stopped. "No," he said, "lend me your hand." He took the doctor's finger and pressed it on the lever.

There was a breath of wind and the lamp flame jumped. The little machine swung round, faded, was seen as a ghost for a second, perhaps, and was gone! Except for the lamp, the table was bare.

Everyone was silent for a minute.

"Look here," said the doctor. "Do you seriously believe that machine has traveled into time?"

"Certainly," said the Time Traveler. "What's more, I have a big machine nearly finished, and when it is ready I mean to try it."

"But if the model has gone into the future we would still see it," I said. "It would be traveling through time just as we are."

"Unless it is traveling much faster than we are," the doctor commented. "Then we would not see it, any more than we see a spoke of a wheel spinning or a bullet flying through the air."

We sat and stared at the empty table.

"Would you like to see the Time Machine itself?" asked the Time Traveler. He picked up the lamp and led us down the hall to his laboratory. There we saw a larger machine just like the little one that had disappeared.

"Look here," said the doctor, "are you serious? Or is this a trick — like the ghost you showed us last Christmas?"

"Upon that machine," said the Time Traveler, holding the lamp aloft, "I intend to explore time. I was never more serious in my life."

None of us quite knew how to take it.

I caught Filby's eyes over the doctor's shoulder. He winked at me solemnly.

I don't think any of us said much about time traveling between that Thursday evening and the next, though we all thought about it a great deal. The following week I went again to Richmond — I was one of the Time Traveler's most constant guests — and found four or five men in his drawing room. The doctor was standing before the fire with a sheet of paper in one hand and a watch in the other.

"It's half-past seven now," said the doctor. "I suppose we'd better have dinner?"

"Where's - - - - -?" I asked, naming our host.

The doctor explained. "It's rather odd. He asked me in this note to lead off with dinner at seven if he's not back. Says he'll explain when he comes."

Only two or three of us had attended the dinner last Thursday. The new guests included an editor and a journalist. During dinner we talked about where our host might be, and I jokingly suggested that he was time traveling. We explained to the others the "trick" we had seen a week before.

As we talked, the door to the hall opened slowly. I saw it first. "Hallo!" I said. "At last!"

The door opened wider and the Time Traveler stood before us.

"Good heavens, what's the matter?" cried the doctor.

The Time Traveler's coat was dirty and smeared with green. His hair was rough and, it seemed to me, grayer. His face was pale, and he looked sick.

He did not speak but came to the table and drank a glass of wine the editor poured for him. Then a ghost of his old smile flickered across his face.

"That's good," he said. His eyes grew brighter. "I'm going to clean up, and then I'll explain things," he said. "Save me some of that mutton. I'm starving for a bit of meat."

He limped out of the room.

"What's the game?" said the journalist. "I don't understand."

"I feel assured it's this business of the Time Machine," I said.

The editor and the journalist made a great joke of that idea.

"I say," said the editor, when our host had returned, "these chaps say you have been traveling into the middle of next week! Tell us about it, will you?"

"I want something to eat first," said the Time Traveler.

We watched while he ate and drank.

"I must apologize," he said at last. "I was simply starving. I've had a most amazing time."

He stood and led us to an adjoining room. "I don't mind telling you the story," he said. "I want to tell it. Most of it will sound like lying, but it's true. . . . I've lived eight days such as no human ever lived before. I'm nearly worn out, so there must be no interruptions. Agreed?"

"Agreed," we said.

And with that he began his story. He sounded tired when he began, but soon he grew excited. At first we glanced now and then at each other, but after a time, as we listened, we looked only at the Time Traveler's face.

TIME TRAVELING

"I told some of you last Thursday about the Time Machine and showed you the thing in my workshop. There it is now, a little travel-worn, but still sound.

"It was at ten o'clock today that the first of all Time Machines began its career. I sat myself in the saddle and took the starting lever in one hand and the stopping one in the other. I pressed one, then the other. I felt as if I were falling, but when I looked around, the laboratory seemed exactly as before. Had anything happened? I looked at the clock. A moment before, as it seemed, it had been ten. Now it was nearly half-past three!

"I drew a breath, gripped the starting lever with both hands, and went off with a thud. The laboratory got hazy. I pressed the lever all the way, and night came like the turning out of a lamp. In another moment came tomorrow. The laboratory grew ever fainter, and day and night followed each other more swiftly than I can tell you.

"I cannot describe the way it feels to travel through time. It is a helpless, headlong feeling, as if one might smash up at any moment. As I went faster, the laboratory fell away, and night followed day like the flapping of a black wing. I saw the moon spinning swiftly, and the sun became a streak of fire. I was still on the hillside where this house stands, but the view had changed. I saw trees grow and fade away. Splendid buildings rose up and passed like dreams. I saw the seasons come and go.

"At last I began to think about stopping. I lugged over

the lever, and I was flung headlong through the air. A clap of thunder filled my ears.

"I landed on soft turf in front of the overturned machine. At first everything seemed gray, but then my head cleared, and I looked around me. I was on a little lawn in a garden, and close by was a great white marble figure, like a sphinx with outspread wings. It stood on a base of bronze and seemed to be looking down at me. Farther away were huge buildings with tall columns.

"I wondered what kind of world I was in. What were men like here? What if they were cruel? What if they thought me some savage animal, only a little like themselves, and killed me?

"Seized with panic, I tried to turn the Time Machine over. I was alone in a strange world, and I felt as a bird may feel, knowing the hawk soars above and will swoop. My fear grew to frenzy. I struggled with the machine, and at last it turned over. One hand on the saddle, the other on the lever, I was ready to mount again.

"But then my courage began to return. I looked less fearfully at this future world. And at that moment I heard voices. Soon a little creature came from the bushes onto the lawn where I stood. He was about four feet high — clad in a purple tunic and wearing sandals. He was very beautiful, but very frail. At the sight of him I suddenly felt braver. I took my hands from the machine.

"In another moment we were face to face, I and this fragile thing out of the future. He laughed into my eyes and did not seem afraid at all. Then he spoke in a strange, sweet tongue to those who followed him.

"Eight or ten of these creatures gathered around me. They touched me to see if I was real, and there was nothing in this that was alarming. But I made a sudden motion to warn them when they tried to touch the Time Machine. At once I removed the little levers that would set the machine in motion and put them in my pocket.

"These little people were as pretty as china dolls. They had curly hair and very tiny ears. Their mouths were small and bright red, the eyes large and mild.

"I tried to talk to them by pointing to myself and the Time Machine. Then I pointed at the sun to suggest passing time. One of the little people made the sound of a clap of thunder, and I realized that he was asking if I had come from the sun in a thunderstorm!

"I was disappointed. Were these creatures fools? I had always believed that the people of the future would be far ahead of us in wisdom, but this question was one a child might have asked.

"Then another little figure came toward me laughing and put a chain of flowers around my neck. Soon they were all flinging flowers upon me — the most wonderful flowers I have ever seen. Then someone suggested that I should be taken to the nearest building, and so I was led past the white sphinx to a huge doorway beyond the garden.

"Many more little people joined us as we entered the building. We were in a great hall lined with low tables of stone. Fruits were heaped on the tables, and there were cushions to sit on while we ate. The hall was very dusty, but the meal of fruit was delightful. I learned later that fruit was all they ate. There were no cattle or sheep in that future world.

"When I had eaten, I decided I must start to learn the language of the little people. I held up a fruit and tried to make them tell me its name. At last they understood, and I soon had learned several words. But my hosts grew tired and wanted to get away from my questions, so I let them give their lessons in little doses. Very little doses they proved to be, for I never met people more easily made tired.

"A queer thing I soon discovered about my little hosts, and that was their lack of interest. Like children, they

would come to me for a while, then wander away after some other toy. When I had eaten, I went outside to look around. I decided to climb a nearby hill from which I could get a wider view of our planet in the year 802701 A.D. For that, I should explain, was the date the dials of my machine recorded.

"I soon realized I was in the valley of the Thames, though the river itself had shifted perhaps a mile from where it is now. There were flowers everywhere, and great heaps of ruins. As I walked, I noticed a pretty little structure like a well with a roof above it, and wondered in passing that there were still wells in the world.

"Glancing back at the little figures following me, I saw that the men and women appeared almost alike. Their lives are so easy, I thought, the men do not have to grow strong to protect their families.

"When I reached the hilltop, I sat down and looked over the valley. It was like one great garden, without hedges or crops. The sunset set me thinking of the sunset of mankind. The people here were the end result of efforts we put forth in the present. All problems of food and health, shelter and clothing had been solved. The air was clear. There were no weeds. The world had become a paradise. And there was no need to be either strong or intelligent when life was so easy. The big buildings were perhaps the last great creations of man, but they were falling into ruin. There was nothing left to do but dance and sing in the sunlight.

"As I stood there in the gathering dark, I thought I understood the whole secret of these beautiful little people. Very simple was my answer, and believable enough — as most wrong ideas are!

A SUDDEN SHOCK

"As I stood there thinking about this too-perfect world, the full moon came up. I shivered and thought I must find a place where I could sleep.

"I looked for the building I knew and the white sphinx. I saw them in the light of the rising moon, and then I found the little lawn where I had landed. I looked at the lawn again. A doubt chilled me.

" 'No,' I said to myself, 'that was not the lawn.'

"But it *was*. You cannot imagine how I felt then, for the Time Machine was gone!

"For a moment I could hardly breathe. Was I trapped in this future world, far from my own time? I ran with great leaping strides down the slope, fell, and fell again. I covered the whole distance from the hilltop to the lawn in ten minutes, crying aloud as I ran. No one answered.

"When I reached the lawn, what I feared was true. Not a trace of the thing was to be seen. I ran about, searching through the bushes, while the sphinx smiled down on me. Then I dashed toward the great building where I had eaten. As I ran, I startled some white animal that, in the dim light, I took for a deer. Inside the building, I lit a match and found a score or so of the little people sleeping.

" 'Where is my Time Machine?' I bawled, like an angry child. Some of them laughed, and most were very frightened. I ran outside again, weeping and raging. How could I have left the machine for even a minute?

"At last I slept, and when I awoke it was full day. In the

freshness of the morning I was more calm. Suppose the machine is destroyed, I thought. I must learn the ways of these people and get materials and tools so that I can make another. It was my only hope.

"But perhaps the machine had only been taken away. I searched the lawn and found signs of where it had been moved. There were queer, narrow footprints nearby. I followed them to the base of the sphinx and rapped on the panels on either side. The base was hollow. I was sure that my Time Machine was inside.

"Two little people came toward me through the bushes. I pointed at the base and showed them that I wished to open the panels. At once they looked very frightened and hurried away. I tried again with another little chap, and he, too, rushed off.

"But I was not beaten. I banged on the panels with my fist. Then I beat on them with a big pebble. I thought I heard a sound like a chuckle from inside, but I must have been mistaken. At last, hot and tired, I sat down to rest.

" 'Patience,' I told myself. 'If you want your machine, you must leave the sphinx alone. Face this world. Learn its ways, and in the end you will find clues to what has happened.'

"Suddenly I saw the humor of this moment. I thought of all the years I had worked to get into the future age, and now I could not wait to get out of it. I had made myself a trap and, although it was at my own expense, I laughed aloud.

"The future world was everywhere as rich as was the Thames valley. From the hilltops I saw spendid buildings, forests, and lakes. Here and there were wells — several, as it seemed to me, of a very great depth. Each was covered over by a little roof. I could see no water in them, but I heard a sound, a thud — thud — thud, like the beating of some big engine. When I threw a scrap of paper into one, it was sucked swiftly out of sight.

"Near the wells were tall towers, and above them was often a flicker in the air such as one sees on a hot day on a sunny beach. I believed the towers to be part of an underground ventilating system, but I could learn nothing about it. In fact, I learned little of the way these people actually lived. For example, I never saw any old or sickly people, and there were no cemeteries. I could find no machinery, no shops. The people spent all their time playing, eating fruit, and sleeping. I could not see how things were kept going.

"The third day I made a friend. I was watching some of the little people bathing in the river, and one of them began drifting away. No one tried to save the crying little thing, and at last I slipped off my clothes, waded in, and caught the poor mite.

"I did not expect gratitude from her, but in that I was wrong. In the afternoon she gave me a big garland of flowers. I was pleased to have a friend, and soon we were seated together talking and smiling. Her name was Weena. That was the beginning of a friendship which lasted a week and ended — as I will tell you!

"She was like a child and wished to follow me everywhere. It was from her I learned that fear had not yet left the world. She was fearless in the daylight, but she dreaded the dark. It set me thinking, and I realized that the little people all gathered into the great houses at night and slept in groups. I never found one outside after dark.

"It must have been the night before Weena's rescue that I was awakened about dawn. I dreamed that I was drowned, and that sea creatures were touching my face. I woke with a start and with a fancy that some grayish animal had just rushed out of the room.

"I could not sleep again, so I rose and went out to see the sunrise. The moon was just setting, and upon the hill I thought I could see white figures like ghosts. Once I saw three of them carrying some dark body. But the light was dim, and I doubted my eyes. Still, I thought about the figures all morning, until Weena's rescue drove them out of my head.

"One very hot morning — my fourth, I think — I sought

shelter in a ruin near the great house where I slept and fed. As I entered a dark room a pair of glowing eyes appeared out of the darkness. I was afraid to turn. Then I thought of my little friends' strange terror of the dark. I stepped forward and put out my hand. I touched something soft, and at once a white apelike figure ran across the sunlit space behind me. It hid in a shadow beneath another pile of ruins.

"What I saw was dull white and had strange large grayish red eyes. There was light hair on its head and down its back. It may have run on all fours, or only with its forearms held very low.

"I followed it and came upon one of those well-like openings of which I have told you. Could this Thing have gone down the shaft? I lit a match and looked down. There was the small white creature looking up at me as it climbed down. It was like a human spider! I saw for the first time that there were metal footrests forming a kind of ladder down the shaft.

"I don't know how long I peered down that well. For a while I could not persuade myself that the Thing was human. At last the truth dawned on me. This future world held two different kinds of people. My little people of the upper world were one; the white dark-loving Thing was the other!

"What was hidden at the foot of that shaft? As I sat there, two beautiful little people came by and were much upset to find me looking into the well. They would not answer my questions and quickly turned away. It seemed to be bad manners to ask about that other world.

"So I had to answer my own questions. And this is what I decided: Beneath my feet must be a world of tunnels which received air from the pillars near the wells. Down there lived the workers who supplied the upper world with clothes and other things they needed. I remembered that in our own day there are railways, workrooms, and shops underground. It appeared that in the future, part of the human race had learned to live underground all the time and had accepted this life. They could not bear the light and would leave their caves only at night.

"It was a frightening idea. The people living above ground without work or challenge had become small in size and intelligence. What had living below ground done to the Morlocks — for that was the name by which these creatures were called?

"Then came many more questions. Why had the Morlocks taken my Time Machine? For I felt sure it was they who had taken it. Why, too, if the upper-world people were the masters, could they not give the machine back to me? Why were they so afraid of the dark? When I tried to ask Weena about the underworld, she burst into tears. They were the only tears, except my own, that I ever saw in the future.

THE MORLOCKS

"The next night I did not sleep well. It occurred to me that the moon must soon pass through its last quarter. As the nights grew dark, the creatures from below would spend more time above ground. I felt restless, like one who is not doing his duty. I felt sure that I could only get back the Time Machine by daring to go underground. But I was afraid to go. If only I had had someone to go with me, it would have been different.

"This restlessness made me wish to explore the world around me. Far off, I had seen a palace of pale green that looked as if it might be made of porcelain. I wished to visit it, but I knew I would only be putting off my visit to the underground world. I decided finally to go down into one of the wells without further delay.

"The shaft was about two hundred yards deep. The climb soon tired me, but I did not dare slow down because the footrests bent under my weight. At last I reached a narrow tunnel in which I could lie down and rest. The air was full of the throb of machinery pumping air down the shaft.

"I do not know how long I lay. I was roused by a soft hand touching my face. I lit a match and saw three stooping white creatures running from the light. I followed them. When I lit another match, I saw that I was in a vast cavern full of great machines. Morlocks were all about me, and there was a smell of fresh blood in the air. In the center of the room was a white table on which lay a great red joint of meat. Then the match burned down and went out.

25

"I have thought since how foolish I was to think men of the future would have everything I might need while I visited them. I had no weapons, not even a camera so that I could take a picture of that terrible underworld. As it was, I stood there with only the powers of hands, feet, and teeth to protect me — and four matches that still remained.

"As I shivered there in the dark, hands plucked at my clothes. I became aware of a bad smell and queer laughing noises. I lit another match and ran back to the narrow tunnel, but I had scarcely entered it when my light went out. I could hear the Morlocks behind me.

"In a moment I was clutched by several hands, and there was no mistaking that they were trying to haul me back. I lit another match to frighten them off and then a third. By that time I had reached the shaft. I found the hooks in the wall, but at that moment my feet were grasped from behind. I lit my last match and kicked hard. Then I pulled loose and climbed swiftly upward. The Morlocks peered up at me — all but one little wretch who followed me for some way.

"The climb seemed endless. I felt faint and sick as I neared the top. At last, however, I staggered out into the sunlight. I fell on my face. I remember Weena there, kissing my hand, and then I fainted.

"Now indeed I seemed worse off than before. Before I had thought I was only held back from finding my Time Machine by the childishness of the little people. Now that I had visited the Morlocks, all had changed. I felt like a beast in a trap, whose enemy would come upon him soon.

"The enemy I dreaded was the darkness of the new moon. Though the Morlocks provided the little people with clothes and other things they needed, there was something else — something terrible that they did under cover of darkness. I did not know what it was, but for some reason there came into my head the memory of the meat I had seen in the underworld. I could not tell why I thought of it then.

"I decided that I must make myself weapons and find a safe place to sleep. I thought then of the palace of green porcelain and decided that might be a safe sleeping place. I set out, with Weena running along beside me, picking flowers to stick in my pockets."

The Time Traveler paused and put his hand into his pocket. He placed two withered flowers upon a table. Then he continued his story.

"Darkness was falling, and there was a thick wood before us. I decided we should pass the night upon an open hill, for the dark wood might be full of dangers. Weena soon slept, but I lay awake. I looked at the stars and thought of the great fear that was between the two kinds of men in this future world. For the first time, with a sudden shiver, I knew what the meat I had seen underground might be. Long ago, the Morlocks must have run out of food. And now they ate the flesh of the little people! My hosts were like cattle which the Morlocks cared for and preyed upon!

"I tried to think about what I must do. I must find a safe place to stay and make myself a weapon. I must find some way to make a fire that would keep the Morlocks away. And I must break down the bronze panels behind which I was sure my machine was hidden. Weena, I decided, I would bring with me to our own time when I found the Time Machine.

"Turning these plans over in my mind the next day, I continued toward the building I had chosen as our home.

"I found the palace of green porcelain to be falling into ruin. Inside was a long gallery that reminded me of a museum, and I soon discovered I was right. In the center of the hall were great dinosaur skeletons covered with dust. At the side were glass cases of fossils.

"Beyond this gallery we found a room full of minerals, then a room of plants and animals, most of which had long since crumbled away. Next was a huge hall of big machines, all rusted and many broken down. Suddenly

Weena came very close to my side. I noticed that the far end of this huge room was very dark, and in that blackness I heard an odd pattering and the same noises I had heard down the well.

"I was about to hurry from the hall when I saw a lever sticking out from one of the machines. I grasped it, and after a minute's strain it snapped off. I had a club that would protect us from any Morlocks we might meet.

"We climbed some stairs to a room full of chemical exhibits, and here, in an airtight case, I found a box of matches. Eagerly I tried them. They were perfectly good!

"In the chemistry room I also found some camphor in a sealed jar. I was about to throw it away but remembered in time that it would burn well and make a good candle. I put it in my pocket. After that I looked in vain for some means of breaking down the bronze panels under the white sphinx. Near the model of a tin mine I found two dynamite cartridges, and for a moment I thought I had the answer to my problem. But they proved to be dummies.

"As evening drew on, we came to a little court within the palace. It had three fruit trees, so we rested and ate. I still had to find a safe place to spend the night, but with the matches and the camphor in my pockets, I was not much troubled. It seemed the best we could do would be to sleep in the open, protected by fire.

"In the morning there would be the getting of the Time Machine to think about. I had not tried to force the bronze panels before, but perhaps with my iron bar I would be able to do so.

IN THE DARKNESS

"I decided we would go as far as possible that night, then build a fire and sleep close to it. I gathered sticks as we walked, but we soon became tired. We moved slowly, and it was full night before we reached the wood. I saw three crouching figures in the bushes and decided that it would be best to try to cross the forest quickly, using the matches and camphor to light the way.

"Still, if I was to hold a lighted match and my iron bar, I would have to put down the firewood I had gathered. Then it came into my head that I would amaze the Morlocks by lighting it. It was a terrible mistake, but at the time it seemed a good idea.

"Weena had never seen fire. She wanted to run to it and play with it. I finally caught her up and carried her off into the wood. For a little way the fire lit the path. Looking back, I saw that the blaze had spread to some bushes.

"Soon I heard a pattering about me. It grew more clear, and then I caught the same queer sounds I had heard in the underworld. The Morlocks were closing in. In another minute I felt a tug at my arm. Weena shivered and became still.

"It was time for a match. I put her down, and at once a struggle began around my knees. When I lit the match the Morlocks fled, but Weena lay clutching my feet. She seemed hardly to breathe. I lit the camphor and flung it to the ground, and as it flared up the Morlocks faded back.

"Weena seemed to have fainted. I picked her up, but

32

now I was horrified to find that I no longer knew in which direction I must go. I had to think rapidly what to do. I decided to build a fire where we were and stay the night.

"I began collecting sticks and leaves. The camphor went out, but I lit a match, and the Morlocks that had been close to Weena dashed away. Soon I had a fire going, but Weena did not wake. I wasn't even sure she breathed.

"I planned to stay awake all night, but the smoke and the camphor smell made me very sleepy. I seemed just to nod and open my eyes — but all was dark. The Morlocks were upon me. Any my matchbox was gone! Little teeth nipped my neck, and soft hands covered me. I felt as if I were in a spider's web. Then my hand came against my iron bar, and, thrusting it about, I was for a moment free.

"I believed that we were lost, but I would make the Morlocks pay dearly for their meat. Suddenly their voices became higher, and I realized they were afraid. The darkness changed. I turned and saw through the nearer trees the flames of the burning forest. It was my first fire coming after me!

"I looked for Weena, but she was gone. The Morlocks were running past me in terror, and I followed them, the flames close behind us.

"And now I was to see the most horrible thing of all I beheld in that future age. This whole space was as bright as day with the light of the fire. In the center was a hill surrounded by burned trees. Beyond this was another arm of the burning forest, with yellow tongues already writhing from it. It encircled the space in a fence of fire.

"The Morlocks were blinded by the light and ran about bumping into each other and into me. Many of them ran straight into the fire! I walked among them, swinging my bar and looking for Weena. But she was gone. I sat down on a small hill and watched the strange company of blind things groping to and fro. They made odd noises as the light of the fire beat on them. I felt I was in a nightmare.

"All that night I waited at a safe distance from the flames and watched the Morlocks blunder about. At dawn I searched again for Weena, in vain. It was plain the Morlocks had left her poor little body in the burning forest, and I would see her no more. At last I climbed a hill and from it was able to see the white sphinx. I knew which way I must walk.

"I was exhausted and full of grief, knowing that I was all alone once more. I began to think of this house of mine, my fireside and friends, and with such thoughts came a longing that was pain.

"But, as I walked over the ashes under the bright morning sky, I made a discovery. In my trouser pocket were still some loose matches. The box must have leaked before it was lost!

"About nine in the morning I came back to the hilltop where I had first sat to look at the world of 802701 A.D. After the terror and grief of the night, it was good to sit in the warm sunlight once more. I found I must sleep.

"I waked a little before sunset and went down the hill to the sphinx. And now came a most unexpected thing. The bronze panels beneath the sphinx were open!

"Within was a small room, and in one corner was the Time Machine. I had the small levers in my pocket. I threw my iron bar away, almost sorry not to use it.

"A sudden thought came to mind as I entered the opening. I knew what the Morlocks planned to do. Sure enough, as I examined the machine, the panels slipped shut, and I was in the dark — trapped. So the Morlocks thought. I chuckled gleefully.

"I could almost hear their laughter as they drew near me. But all I had to do was fasten the lever in place and depart like a ghost. However, I had overlooked one thing. My matches were of the kind that light only on the box!

"You can imagine how I felt then. The little brutes were

all about me. I scrambled into the saddle of the machine and pushed them away as I felt for the studs that held the levers in place. One of the levers slipped from my hand, and I had to butt in the dark with my head — I could hear a Morlock's skull ring — to get it back. It was a nearer thing than the fight in the forest, this last scramble.

"But at last the lever was in place and pulled over. The clinging hands slipped away. Darkness fell from my eyes, and I found myself in the same gray light I have told you about before.

THE FURTHER VISION

"I have already told you of the sickness and strain that come with time traveling. This time I was not seated well in the saddle and had to cling to the machine as it swayed. When I looked at the dials, I was amazed to see how far I had traveled. One dial shows days, another thousands of days, another millions, and another thousands of millions. I had pulled the levers forward, and when I looked at the dials I saw the thousands hand sweeping around as fast as the second hand of a watch — into the future.

"Carefully, I brought the machine to a stop. I was on a bleak moorland covered with green plants. The great buildings were all gone, and even the shape of the land had changed.

"Suddenly a dark bulk rose out of the moor, then disappeared into a valley. Close by, I saw many faint-gray things moving about. They hopped like kangaroos and had straight grayish hair. When I brought one of them down with a rock, I found it strangely human. The hands, the roundish head, and the eyes gave it a somewhat human look. As I knelt looking at the thing, the great bulk I had seen earlier drew close, and the small animals scattered. What I saw was a monster, something like a centipede but perhaps thirty feet long! It was coming quite fast and left me little time to mount my machine and ride on into the future.

"The gray world grew darker, and the changes from day to night grew slower, though I was traveling very fast. At

last there was only twilight. The sun rose and fell in the west, and there was no trace of the moon. The earth had come to rest with one face to the sun.

"I stopped gently and sat upon the Time Machine, looking around. The sky was no longer blue. Northeastward it was inky black, and out of the blackness shone steadily the pale stars. Overhead it was a deep red and starless. Southeastward it was a glowing scarlet where, cut by the horizon, lay the huge red hull of the sun. The rocks around me were of a reddish color, and were partly covered by a bright green vegetation. It was the same green one sees on plants in caves: plants like these which grow in perpetual twilight.

"The machine was standing on a sloping beach. The sea rose and fell like a gentle breathing. Along the edge of the water was a thick crust of salt — pink under the red sky. My head ached, and I noticed that I was breathing very fast. I judged the air to be thinner than it is now.

"Far away I heard a harsh scream, and saw a thing like a huge white butterfly go fluttering up into the sky. Looking around me, I saw that what I had taken to be a rock was moving slowly towards me. It was really a monstrous crab-like creature, as big as a table. As I stared at it, I felt a tickling on my cheek. I struck at it, and caught something threadlike. I turned, and saw that I had grasped the antenna of another monster crab just behind me. In a moment my hand was on the lever, and I had flown away.

" So I traveled, in great strides of a thousand years or so, watching the sun grow duller and the life of the old earth ebb away. Thirty million years hence I stopped once more on the beach. It was bitter cold, with fringes of ice along the shore. Now and again white flakes came floating down. I saw no movement or life at all. To the northeast I could see the glare of pinkish white snow under the black sky.

"Suddenly a bay appeared in the side of the sun. It rapidly grew larger, and I knew an eclipse was beginning.

The darkness grew, the breeze rose to a moaning wind, and the sky was absolutely black.

"A horror of this great darkness came on me. I felt sick. Then, like a red-hot bow in the sky, appeared the edge of the sun. I saw something moving against the red water of the sea. It was round, with tentacles trailing from it, and it hopped fitfully about. I felt I was fainting, but the fear of lying helpless in that awful twilight helped me to fly away on my machine.

"So I came back. For a long time I knew nothing; then the change from night to day began again and the sun became golden once more. The land changed its shape again and yet again, as the hands on the dials spun backward. At last I began to see the shadows of houses, and soon after that the buildings began to look the way they do today. Then the old walls of the laboratory came around me. I stopped the machine.

"I got off the thing very shakily and sat down upon my bench. I trembled for a while but gradually became calmer. The whole journey might have been a dream.

"Yet not exactly. The machine had started in the southeast corner of the laboratory and was now in the northwest. That gives you the exact distance from the little lawn where I landed to the base of the white sphinx where the Morlocks had carried my machine.

"Presently I came here. I saw the newspaper by the door and found the day was indeed today and the hour almost eight. I heard your voices and sniffed good wholesome meat. I opened the door on you, and you know the rest. I washed and dined, and now I am telling you the story.

"This must seem very strange to you," he said after a pause. "But to me the one strange thing is that I am safely back. What do you think of it all?"

The editor stood up with a sigh. "What a pity you're not a writer of stories!" he said.

"You don't believe it? I thought not." The Time Traveler

looked at the withered flowers on the table. "I can hardly believe it myself. Did I make a Time Machine? Was it a dream?" He caught up the lamp and hurried down the hall to his laboratory. We followed him. The machine was there, with brown spots and bits of moss on it.

"Yes, it *is* all true," the Time Traveler said. We returned in silence to the room where we had heard his story.

That night I could not sleep, and the next day I went back to the Time Traveler's house. His laboratory was empty, but I met him in the hall carrying a camera and a knapsack. He laughed when he saw me.

"I know why you came," he said. "Give me half an hour, and I will prove to you that I can travel in time. Will you wait?"

I waited in the drawing room, until suddenly I remembered that I had promised to meet a friend for lunch. I went to the laboratory to tell the Time Traveler.

As I opened the door, a gust of air whirled around me. The Time Traveler was not there. I seemed to see a ghostly figure in a whirling mass of black and brass for a moment, and then it was gone. The Time Machine was gone, too.

Then I understood. At the risk of disappointing my friend, I stayed on, waiting for the Time Traveler to return with another, perhaps still stranger story. Maybe he would bring photographs with him.

Only now I am beginning to fear I must wait a lifetime. The Time Traveler vanished three years ago. And as everybody knows, he has never returned.

EPILOGUE

Will he ever return? Has he fallen among savages or dinosaurs? Or has he gone only a little way into the future where the riddles of our own time are answered and its worst problems solved?

Long before the machine was made, the Time Traveler told me he did not think cheerfully of the future. He was afraid that we would destroy ourselves in the end. If that is so, we must live as though it were not so. And I have by me, for my comfort, two strange flowers — brown and flat now — to witness that even when mind and strength had gone, gratitude and love still lived on in the heart of man.

GLOSSARY

camphor (kam′ fər)   a strong-smelling chemical taken from the camphor tree

eclipse (i klips′)   when the sun or moon is hidden by the shadow of another heavenly body

fossil (fahs′ əl)   the remains of a plant or animal that lived in past ages

journalist (jərn′ əl əst)   a person who gathers news and makes it public

laboratory (lab′ rə tōr ē)   a place for doing science experiments

porcelain (pōr′ sə lən)   a hard, thin kind of pottery

sphinx (sfingks)   a statue with the head of a person and the body of a lion

ventilate (vent′ əl āt)   to change stale air for fresh air